CONTENT WARNINGS

Please note that this is a work of erotica, not romance, that heavily focuses on breeding fantasies. This book contains an age gap relationship between a monster and a human and is intended for readers over 18.

Non-exhaustive list of content/triggers: Heavy breeding kink (unprotected sex), dubcon, fated mates, primal kink, dirty talk, lactation kink (adult nursing fantasies), monster x human, size difference, unusual monster peen and other anatomy, pregnancy including pregnant sex, public sex, monster babies, and typos and grammatical errors.

This is a work of fiction featuring imaginary scenarios. Do not try this at home. Only read if you are comfortable with the above themes. The author does not endorse the beliefs or actions of the characters.

CHAPTER 1
ESMERALDA

"It's your turn to clean the master's room tonight," Alice, the housekeeper says to me. Her voice echoes in the humongous stone castle with high ceilings, one that is built for a dragon.

"The master's room?" I shudder underneath my plain brown gown. It's been two weeks since I started working at Blaze's castle and I'd be stupid if I weren't afraid of my dragon master. Everyone in the village fears him. He's a powerful dragon, not to mention an extremely wealthy one, who could end the whole village with a single breath. If it weren't for my brother's debt, I wouldn't be working here. This place pays more than any other establishment in the village, but it's also like walking a tightrope. Blaze's castle is a legend in the village. To maintain the peace, humans go work for him, but they all know better than to annoy him. There are rumors that he once breathed fire and reduced a maid to ashes for touching his valuable baubles.

"That's right. It's your turn today." Alice glares at me. We all take turns cleaning the master's room while he's out bathing in the stream adjoining the castle land. There are acres of trees and grass around Blaze's home, which he also owns. Cleaning Blaze's room is a tricky thing because one little mistake and I could be burned to ashes.

My nipples tighten at the thought of the majestic dragon I glimpsed when I first arrived here. While cleaning the baths, I accidentally stumbled upon him bathing and stood there gaping for hours. With his shining yellow eyes, large snout, and tiny ears, he's a force to be reckoned with. Blaze is over a hundred years old, with the most magnificent iridescent purple scales covering his body. His sheer size is impressive. He must be at least four times as big as a human, with a long tail that made my insides flutter. But that wasn't what had me staring for so long. It was the monster between his legs. When Blaze emerged from the bath, I saw his bare cock, hanging large and heavy between his legs. I swallowed hard at the sight of a purple penis, throbbing and hard, my pussy immediately clenching in response. God, it was so beautiful, hard like a purple velvet pole and curved, an apple-shaped knot pulsing at the base. I know dragons can breed humans, but I can't even imagine that thing fitting into me. My pussy, on the other hand, dripped for my dragon master, excited by the possibility of accommodating that monster.

I quickly turned away before he could see me and ran. When I reached my room, I glimpsed at myself in the mirror, my heart thudding in my chest. There's no way a beautiful monster like that would ever look at me with desire. With a round face, dull brown eyes, and a plump body, I'm considered homely at best. Even back in the village, none of the men were interested in me. That's why my family sent me to work for Blaze, knowing I had no marriage prospects anyway. I send the money I earn back home and get to live in this castle instead. I touched my

THE DRAGON'S MAID

JADE SWALLOW

Copyright © 2024 by Jade Swallow

All rights reserved.

No part of this book may be reproduced in any form or by any electronic or mechanical means, including information storage and retrieval systems, without written permission from the author, except for the use of brief quotations in a book review.

CONTENTS

Content Warnings	v
1. Esmeralda	1
2. Blaze	9
3. Esmeralda	18
4. Blaze	27
5. Esmeralda	35
6. Esmeralda	45
About the Author	51
Also by Jade Swallow	53

cheek, surveying my bound brunette hair. The brown gown clung awkwardly to my motherly curves, making me look even more drab. With a sigh, I got back to work. Fantasies weren't for a girl like me.

"I'll do it." My words to Alice are fraught with determination. I've never cleaned Blaze's room before, but how hard can it be? I'll just do my job and get out as soon as possible.

Alice thrusts the broom and dusting cloth into my hand, saying, "Make sure the room is spotless. Our master hates shoddy work."

Yes, ma'am." My heart hammering in my chest, I make my way upstairs. Blaze's castle is spic and span, just the way he likes it. With gigantic crystal chandeliers decorated with a thousand candles, the area next to the wide, winding staircase looks like a dream. I climb the stony stairs that could fit six of me, and gaze at the blue skies outside the tall, arched windows. Glass lamps decorate either side of the main staircase. I feel like a princess as I descend the stairs, and I wonder how it'd feel like to be the lady of this castle. My heart flutters with each step, my imagination growing deeper. The lady would not only get to live a life of luxury in this beautiful castle, but she'd also have the privilege of warming Blaze's bed and bearing his heirs.

I swallow when I reach the landing. Blaze has never shown any interest in a human or dragon. There are dragons in other villages, but there have been no rumors of a marriage. They say dragons can only mate with their fated mate, which is why it's important they find them. Dragons are rare creatures and they need to mate and breed to increase their numbers. As I walk through the wide hallway, I imagine what it'd feel like to be a dragon's mate, its breeding vessel. The thought of that purple tail touching my clit and playing with my pussy is enough to make me want to sign up. There's just something about Blaze that has me wanting ever since the day I saw him.

The master suite is the largest in the castle. I turn the knob that's as big as my head and make my way in. The door is wide and tall, made for a dragon, not a human. The moment I step into the chamber, I gasp. Everything in it is dragon-sized. The master bed occupying half the room is enough to fit two dragons. I have no idea how Blaze ever managed to find a mattress that size, but I know it's my job to clean it. The white sheets over it are rumpled. I've washed sheets that size before, but I never thought someone actually slept on a bed that huge. There are glasses that come up to my knee and a water jug that's all the way up to my waist. The rug stretches for miles. There's another room inside his bedroom, which is his hoard of jewels. He has many of them, with a particular preference for pearls and rubies. None of the maids are allowed into that room.

I move to the mantle, gazing at a row of objects that have dust on them. Has it been that long since Blaze's room has been cleaned? I reach out for the first item, deciding to begin my task there. It's a small trinket box made of gold and pink lacquer. I touch it gently, moving my cloth over it to dust its surface. Once I'm done, I put it back, shiny like new. The next thing is curious. It's a glass jar with a little blue bottle inside that seems to be filled with some sort of liquid. It's exotic, which makes me curious. I touch the glass, trying to pick it up, but as soon as I touch it, I realize that it's hot.

"Oww." I retract my hand too quickly unbalancing the glass case. It wobbles and before I can react, falls down. A loud crash resounds as the glass shatters to pieces, releasing the blue glass tube of potion. It breaks, and all of a sudden, blue fumes burst into the room. I cough, shielding my eyes, trying to protect myself from the assault of gas, but it's too much. My body is burning up, my stomach contracting, and my eyes watering. I feel a deep need rise inside my core, one that I've suppressed for twenty-three years of my existence. Damn, this is the worst time to be feeling aroused. Once Blaze finds out what I've done, he's going to be furious.

While I am trying to fan the fumes away, I hear the door open. All of a sudden, the fumes whoosh out. As the haze clears, I stop coughing. Instead, I stare up at the massive shadow that stands next to the door. Yellow eyes shine, making me shiver in fear. There's no doubt about who he is. Blaze's claws cut through the fog, his heavy voice coughing. As the last of the fumes fade away, I'm left staring at my dragon master.

Looking down on me from up close, he's bigger than I remember. His wings unfurl behind him, taking up half the room. Blaze's gleaming black claws are unsheathed, ready to tear me to pieces. He growls, revealing his sharp white teeth that are as large as my nose.

Oh my god, he's going to burn me to ashes.

"Who broke my love potion?" He growls, glaring down at me. My tiny body shivers under him, an odd mix of fear and arousal coloring my blood. He smells like pine, man, and fire burning on a slow winter night. And I can't stop my pussy from growing damp at the sight of him. His monster penis is naked and throbbing, his growls growing louder. I can see his organ swelling with the need. The veins decorating its surface make my mouth go dry. Oh my god, I just summoned an aroused dragon, thanks to my clumsiness, and he's angry.

"I'm sorry…" My voice is hysterical as I take a step away from my master. He steps in, shutting the door with a thud loud enough to rattle my bones. Then, he approaches me, filling the space between us in a single stride. His tail drags on the floor, his wings moving slightly as he gazes down at me with his liquid gold eyes and a serpent-like long iris. My body is burning like a furnace, so undeniably into my master. He might be scary, but he's a beautiful monster. I can't take my eyes off him. "I didn't know it was so hot…"

I stop moving when the bag of my thighs hits the bed. Blaze extends his hand forward and grips my shoulder. When his scaly fingers brush against my skin, I feel a spark deep in my belly. He leans forward, his snout touching my cheek. It's wet and warm, his breaths misting against my skin and slipping through the hem of my gown to my aroused nipples. His touch makes me turn to liquid.

In a deep voice, Blaze asks, "What's your name, little maid?"

"Esmeralda…" I answer, fear coating my senses.

"I've never seen you before." His voice sounds gentle, almost conversational. I lose my balance and fall on the bed, the mattress padding my back. Within seconds, Blaze is on top of me, pinning me down.

"I…just started working here two weeks ago…" My eyes flood with tears, even as my body begs for Blaze's touch.

"And why did you come to work for me?" he asks. "Everyone in the village is afraid of me."

"I…really need the money. My family is in debt," I honestly answer. "If you let me live, I promise to pay back your kindness."

"Let you live?" He snorts. "Do you know what the thing you broke was?"

I shake my head. "A love potion meant for my mate.

When I met my mate, I was going to give it to her to make our joining easier."

"What?" My jaw drops. I know how important mating is to dragons. I can't believe I messed up so bad.

"I'm so sorry..." My voice is shaky as he climbs above me, his monstrous form pinning me down. His wings unfurl, his snout sniffing my neck and breasts. "I will do anything to make up for my mistake."

"Anything?" The way his eyes glint makes a frisson of thrill race up my spine.

"Anything." This is the only way I can live. Whatever he plans to do to me can't be worse than death.

"The potion you just broke sent me into a heat. The moment I inhaled it and saw your fertile body standing there, there was only one thing I wanted to do."

"What?" I know the answer, but I still ask. Dragons only go into a heat when they're ready to breed. Ideally, it happens once they meet their mate, but that is clearly not what happened here. The blue fumes must've triggered his heat. Once they're in heat, though, they don't stop fucking their mate until they've bred here.

Blaze sniffs my breasts, his meaty shaft pressing against my belly. It's huge, dripping purple liquid all over my dress. My fingers touch his shimmering scales and I feel a jolt of arousal skewer my core. Oh my god, am I in heat too? I mean, humans can't go into heats, but the need thrumming through my veins, making my blood burn, can't be explained by anything else. My nipples are hard as rocks, aching to break free of the confines of my dress. I need this monster to breed me so bad. My entire body is on fire. He runs his claws over my breasts, gazing down at me. "You feel it too, don't you? Your body wants me."

"Yes...you're so beautiful." It's an honest answer.

Blaze smiles. "It looks like you're ready to pay for your crimes, then."

Blaze doesn't waste any time. His body must be as needy as mine. With a single swipe of his fingers, he rips my gown in two. I scream as the air hits my aroused nipples, making them hard before my dragon employer's gaze.

"Lie back, Esmeralda, I'm going to breed you tonight."

CHAPTER 2
BLAZE

Esmeralda is a sight for sore eyes. Her gown parts from the middle to reveal her lush curves. I rip the fabric into pieces, leaving nothing between us. She moans in delight as her body is bared to me, the cool air hitting her hard nipples and making them bead.

My new maid is all curves, her soft magnolia skin making my cock harder. I've been waiting for my mate for a hundred years, and finally, she's here. Esmeralda doesn't know that I've been watching ever since she spied on me during my bath. I followed my tempting new maid out that day, mesmerized by the sway of her curvy hips. The way her big tits and ass jiggled as she ran away made me want to chase her down and claim her. Just the scent of her aroused my cock into dripping pre-cum in the bath. Does she know how much I want her? Does she sense my need for her? One whiff of her scent, and I knew she was the one. But I held back, just watching her go about her duties every day instead.

There's a prophecy in my clan. Dragons in my family find their mate by accident. When I was young, my parents went to a dragon astrologer, who said whoever broke my love potion would be my mate. He gave me a tube of blue potion and said I must store it carefully. When it's time for me to mate, my fated one will find me and will end up accidentally breaking the glass.

From the moment I saw Esmeralda, everything in my body responded. I wanted her to find and break my greatest treasure, tying us together in a fated bond. Every time I secretly watched her tending to the gardens outside or secretly watching me, I felt an odd thrill. Blood rushed through my body, aching to mate my beautiful, fertile human.

That's why I placed the love potion where it could be easily found and broken, and asked the housekeeper to send her to clean my rooms. I was tired of waiting.

Sure enough, Esmeralda fulfilled the prophecy by breaking the glass and sending me into a heat. There's no going back from this now. I've waited a hundred years to meet her, and now that she's under me, I'm not going to stop until her belly is swollen with my heirs. As a powerful dragon, it's my duty to produce as many heirs as possible to expand our population.

"I know you've been watching me in the bath, Esmeralda," I say to her, touching her soft tits. They're so plump, firm, and round, that I want to put my mouth on them and suckle her rosy tips. My mate is not thin and frail like other women. She's plump and beautiful, her face radiant like the moon. Every time she walks, she makes my heart beat faster.

"What...I..." Her dark eyes meet mine, searching for an excuse. The way she bites on her lush lower lip makes me want to kiss her. "I...I didn't mean you to find out. It's just that...you're so beautiful. I couldn't stop looking at you. I'm sorry."

"Don't be sorry." I retract my claws, brushing Esmeralda's pebbled pink peak with my touch fingers. Mine are much larger than her human ones, but I relish the feel of her hard bud pebbling under my skin. "Why didn't you tell me you were attracted to me?"

"How could I?" Her voice turns into a moan when I brush her peak harder. My palms cup her sweet, plump tits and knead those globes of fat, loving how her entire body shakes in response. Her round, heavy mounds are tiny in my hands, but I love the way they feel to grab. "You're my master. I'm a servant with debts. How could I even think about being with you?"

I know that she's here to make money to pay her family's debts. I flew down to the village and watched her family. I know her brother is deep in debt, and they're all struggling to pay it back. Once I claim Esmeralda, I will pay back their debt so that my human mate never has to worry.

"You're so tempting, little human." I slide my fingers down her skin, touching her lush hips. They're full of fat, fertile, and curvy, perfect for bearing my children. She's no frail female who will crash under the weight of a dragon's body. No, she's the perfect curvy companion, her body created to grow and nourish my children. I knew it the moment I saw her.

My tail flicks on her other nipple, making her moan wildly.

"Oh my god..." The tip of my tail circles her rosy peak and plays with it, pulling and rolling it, while my fingers do the same to the other one. I tease them to hard points, putting my mouth on one and suckling when she's ready for me. Her nipples taste so sweet, disappearing like cotton candy under my forked tongue. I bet they'll be even sweeter when her tits and plump and filled with milk. Esmeralda's hands wind around my neck, teasing my scales as she clings harder to me and feeds me her sweet tits. I roll my tongue over her peak and suck, teasing her peak with my teeth. "You feel so good..."

My tail slithers down her body, loving the feel of her soft skin, and touches her wet pussy. She's soaked thanks to the effects of the drug and our foreplay. I tease her puffy folds with my scaly tail, the friction making her moan louder.

"You're so wet," I whisper against her tit, suckling the other nipple gently. "Are you aching for cock?"

"Yes!" She cries out when I suckle her other peak, making her gush more honey from those soft folds. She's so delicate there, so perfect to breed. My tail flicks on her clit and she arches her back, her cries echoing in my bedroom. The huge bed eats her up, making my human mate look more vulnerable. Using my tail, I tease her wet bud, assaulting it and circling it until she's crying out for more.

Pulling my mouth off her pink nipple, I gaze down at her fertile, naked body, writhing under me. My snout sniffs her skin, traveling up to her mouth. I press a kiss on her soft lips, feeling an electric shock right down to my toes. Esmeralda opens her mouth for me, and though it's much smaller than mine, it fits perfectly against my contours. I kiss her, tasting her sweet flavor. When my long, forked tongue thrusts into her mouth, she doesn't resist, enjoying the way our tongues mate. Her naked body pressed against mine is a delicious temptation that makes my cock grow harder. I can smell her sweet pussy producing honey. My tail circles her dripping cunt, and I slide the tip in.

I drink Esmeralda's cries with my mouth, deepening the

kiss and claiming my princess. Her fingers slide over the rim of my wings and my cock twitches against her thigh. It's my most sensitive part, and the fact that my mate is caressing it makes it special. My tail slides in deeper into her cunt, testing the temperature. Her cries deepen, but I don't remove my mouth from hers. Her pussy is warm and fleshy, perfect for breeding.

I tear my mouth away from hers, gazing down at her beautiful, round face that is flushed. I lean back and push her thighs apart, stunned at the sight of her dripping pussy. Pulling my tail out of her cunt, I touch it with my fingers. "Such a pretty pussy." I stroke her glistening folds, loving how sensitive they are. "Look how you're quivering for your mate." I gaze into her eyes and know she's hungry for cock. "Are you ready to be bred, Esmeralda?"

"Yes." Her entire body is shaking in anticipation of our mating. I'm going to knot and breed her tonight, and she knows it. "I want your cock, Blaze."

I love how she says my name. I can't deny my mate any longer. I bring the tip of my huge cock to her entrance and rub my pre-cum all over her folds. It's going to help her take my massive breeding organ. We have a huge size difference and I have no doubt that tight cunt is going to milk me dry. My knot pulses at the base of my erect cock, eager to get acquainted with my mate.

"Lie back, princess. I'm going to take care of your body." I push her back on the bed, covering her with my body. Then, I position my cock on her cunt and push in.

"Aahhh..." Pleasure skewers her body as I penetrate her fleshy cavern. Her wet walls expand around me, gripping me hard as I drive deeper into her.

"Damn, you're so tight, little one." Heat blooms at the

base of my spine. I love the sight of my veiny purple cock sinking into her pink pussy.

"You're so big..." she says, her hands reaching up to grip my wings. That increases my pleasure, making my balls ache with the need to unload my seed into her baby-making vessel. I dig my fingers into her fat hips, holding her as I thrust into her. My long, slithering tongue shoots out and licks her nipples, the forked end curving around one and rolling it around.

"Oh...that feels so good..."

I drive home with one final thrust, seating myself deep inside my mate's pussy. She's all around me, drenching my cock with her scent and juices. I feel her hard nipples on my tongue, her curvy, fleshy body panting under my legs. My knot hangs outside her pussy. I'll give it to her when I'm ready to breed her. For now, I just want to admire the sight of her stuffed with my cock, her body so beautifully naked under me. I am huge, four times her size, my purple, scaly monster body a contrast to her soft, human one.

"Good girl," I whisper. "Look at how good you take my cock."

"Mmmm...my pussy is so full of cock," she says. "You feel so good inside me."

"I'm going to make you feel even better," I say, moving my hips. I pull out my cock and thrust it back into her, making her entire body jerk. Her big tits jiggle violently as I slam into her fertile pussy, going deep.

"Oh..." A jolt of pleasure skewers her body as I begin fucking my mate. In another world, I would take her tenderly and kiss her while I slowly made love to her body, but the potion triggered my heat. I can't control myself. I drive into her like a deranged monster, every thrust, making the need in my balls grow. "Yes...don't stop...harder…" My cock drills her pussy ruthlessly, driven by the instinct to breed. Esmeralda is submissive, giving herself to my lovemaking.

My big balls slap her ass as I grind into her deeper, assaulting her sweet spot with the tip of my purple cock. My whiskers tickle her skin as I bury my snout in her breasts, licking and nibbling on them while my cock destroys her pussy. The friction is driving me crazy. I grind my knot against her channel, ready to mate.

"I'm going to knot you, Esmeralda," I growl against her skin. "I'm going to plug up your pussy and fill your womb with my seed." My fingers trace her soft stomach. "You'll be swollen with my baby in no time."

My huge, distended knot slips into her channel and she cries out loud. It's too much for her. Humans weren't made to take big dragon knots, but my mate does so well. "Just a little more, baby. Take me in."

"Oh…I've never been stretched so much before…" Her soft voice disappears as my knot enters her cunt. I continue fucking her, grinding my ball of flesh into her pussy. Her inner walls grip me hard, making me want to spurt cum into her fertile womb.

"I'm going to come." Her voice is tight as my body rocks into her entrance. "I can't…hold it anymore."

"Come for me." I kiss her cheek. I can feel her body shaking under mine, so close to the climax. I don't stop drilling her, grinding her insides with my big knot until she's coming apart in my arms.

With a loud shriek, my maid climaxes. Her inner walls spasm and grip my cock so hard that she chokes me into releasing my seed.

"Damn," I growl as my orgasm seizes me simultaneously. My knot locks into place, plugging up her pussy as my cock ejects ropes of thick semen into her belly. The tightness in my balls explodes as my core blazes with pleasure. Her walls massage my dick and milk more cum out of me. I dump my load into her, stuffing her small body with my baby-making seed. There's so much of it that it makes her stomach bloat, giving the image that she's already carrying my baby.

I squeeze her round, firm tits, making her scream as waves of ecstasy wash upon her. I'm drowning too, right there with her. The deep need that's been pulsing inside my groin for hours finally calms down as I breed Esmeralda and mate her. I kiss her skin, licking and tasting every inch of that perfect body. She's mine now. I've claimed her, and I'm not going to let her go.

I continue coming inside her until she's milked every last drop of my seed. When the orgasm lets up, I collapse against her. I put my arms around my mate, holding her close to my chest where my heart beats. My knot is still stuck inside her pussy, and it's going take two hours before I'm ready to disengage.

"Wow." Her voice is breathy. She looks down at her stomach, caressing its bloated surface. "That was amazing. I never thought we'd come together so perfectly." Her eyes are shiny when she looks up at me. My heart beats faster. I need to tell her that she's my mate, that I plan to marry and keep breeding her for the rest of my life. "Thank you. It was the perfect first time."

"First time?" My heart clenches. "You waited for me?"

It heartens me to know that my mate saved herself for me.

"Well, I was unpopular in the village. I'm not considered a beauty, as you know. No one ever wanted me."

"Rubbish." I slip my fingers under her chin and hold it

up. "You're the most beautiful woman I've ever met. You're the one I've waited a hundred years for."

She inhales deeply, and the tears begin to flow. "I know I'm not good enough for you, but thank you for thinking that way about me. What we shared was the most special moment of my life, I'll never forget it. You made me feel so desired."

I wipe her tears, kissing her head. "Don't cry, Esmeralda. You're a precious gem. Mere humans can't see your value. You were meant to be a dragon's bride."

"Bride?" She sniffs and looks up, stroking my cock inside her belly. "You can't mean…"

"Now that I've bred you, there's only one thing left to do," I whisper against her skin. "I'm going to marry you."

CHAPTER 3
ESMERALDA

I feel like a princess in a red velvet gown. With a square-cut neck that reveals the tops of my fat tits, and a bodice that hugs my waist and wide hips, it is a work of art. Blaze got it made for me after our night together, and it fits my body like a glove. I'm having dinner with him tonight. He said I was to dress up and present myself in the dining hall at eight. Maids were sent to my room to dress me up, and this gown was delivered earlier this morning. The tailor made little adjustments, and now, it's ready.

It's been three days since Blaze bred me. After he took me to his bed, we ended up making love through the night. His heat was gone when the sun surfaced the next morning, and I'd been filled with his seed several times over. I stroke my belly that's still flat, hoping it'll soon swell up with my dragon master's child.

Turning my face to the mirror, I notice the newfound glow on my face. I've been filled with joy ever since Blaze made love to me. After his heat ended, he instructed me that I was to come to his room every night so that he could continue breeding me. We've been doing that for the last two days, and every night, he says he wants to marry me. But I can't accept his offer.

I notice my dull brown eyes in the mirror and remind myself that I'm nothing but a maid. It's my privilege to be a breeding vessel for my master, but we can never be anything more. Blaze is a wealthy dragon who lives in this beautiful castle, and I'm a poor maid with debts to pay. Though I may daydream about becoming the lady of the castle, I know that Blaze is too good for me. How can I ever hope to be his equal when all I can give him is my love?

My heart aches with the need to say yes. There's nothing I'd love more than to spend the rest of my days with my dragon. I never thought I'd be so attracted to a monster, but it seems that I was always waiting for Blaze. I can't imagine being attracted to a human now. From the first moment I laid eyes on him, I knew he was special. When he bred me the first night, something inside me started to beat again. It's like I was always meant to find him, always meant to be with him.

"The master is waiting for you," a maid opens the door, staring at me. I know it's Priscilla, a girl I used to work with. Her eyes skim my gown, and I know she's wondering why I'm suddenly getting special treatment. Do the other maids resent me for sleeping with the master? After all, I only got a chance to sleep with him because I messed up and broke the tube of blue potion. If it hadn't been for that, I might still be polishing wood and opening doors.

Stuffing my worries inside, I step out of the room, making sure not to ruin my gown. My hair is arranged in an intricate hairdo, grown tendrils slipping out of my bun. I look beautiful in my new clothes and makeup, and I know Blaze has gone out of this way to make me feel like a princess. I've never felt so beautiful in twenty-three years of my life as I have in the last three days. Blaze's gaze, his touch, and his attention make me feel like the most special woman in the world.

"Miss Esmeralda." My name is announced when I step into the dining room. Blaze is sitting at the head of the table, his beautiful purple scales on display. He's always breathtaking, so big and majestic. He takes up the entire room with his charismatic presence. I can't breathe when I look at him. My heart aches with longing. I want to cry because I can't marry him. All because I was not born his equal. Through the fog of my longing, I know without a doubt that I'm in love with him.

"Good evening." His deep voice makes dark desires awaken in my belly. Blaze motions to his servants who guide me to a seat at the end of the table. It's much smaller than his, raised to meet the height of the table. A beautiful white tablecloth covers the massive 16-seater, glass goblets and china laid out on its surface along with a display of blue hydrangeas and red roses. It's like a fairytale—dining in a castle as old as Blaze's. Everything is crafted to perfection. "You look stunning. I wish I could ravish you instead of my dinner."

A bubble of joy expands in my heart at the compliment. My pussy is already warm, ready to submit to her master. "Thank you. I feel like I'm in a dream." The words come tumbling out of my mouth when the manservant moves away. Blaze's yellow eyes are on mine. I always lose myself in them. They're so different from human eyes but so mesmerizing. "Everything here is so beautiful...thank you, I feel so blessed to be dining with you."

"It's what you deserve. Sit down and enjoy yourself. Tonight is all about you." My dragon master says. Blaze doesn't wear clothes because he's a dragon, but the yellow light spilling from the three-tier crystal chandelier makes his purple scales shine. I've never met a creature as beautiful as him. Every time I look at him, I'm captivated anew.

Blaze snaps his fingers and the footmen appear with food. A bowl of soup is placed in front of me and then the footmen disappear.

"Eat, my dear. I hope you enjoy everything tonight."

I pick up the spoon and taste some of the rich cream of mushroom soup. The moment the mix of umami and saltiness hits my tongue, I moan. Blaze raises his gaze to me, enjoying watching my expressions as I consume the bowl of soup in an instant. I've only ever smelled the food cooked in the kitchen and wondered what it'd taste like. Every time I watched the rich displays be served to our master and his guests, I could only fantasize about being in a place like this. But now, it's a reality. I plan to enjoy every moment of tonight. Blaze picks up his bowl, which is five times the size of mine, and empties it into his mouth like a toy teacup.

"This is delicious." I put the spoon aside and watch the father of my soon-to-be kid. He must be the most handsome dragon in the world. Maybe it's my hormones, but I love the way he looks at me, his mouth opening in question. I wouldn't choose anyone else to impregnate me. That's for sure. The pleasure Blaze makes me feel is unparalleled.

The main course is brought on and I devour it. The pregnancy has made me hungry.

"I can't believe I get to eat rich foods like this," I mumble between courses.

"Slow down," Blaze says. "You can have as much as you want." There's a light in his eyes as he watches me eat with amusement. I wish all my evenings could be like this, sitting across this mesmerizing monster and being watched by him.

When we get to the dessert, Blaze asks his staff to leave. We're left alone in the massive dining room, lights glinting all around.

"Thank you for this magical night," I tell him. "This is like a fairytale. Everything is so exquisite, and the food was great."

Blaze gets off his chair and walks to me. "You don't have to thank me. From today on, this is the treatment you're going to get every day."

He leans closer and plants a kiss on my head. My entire body sparks like a live wire, his kiss making me come alive.

"Marry me. Esmeralda." His commands echo in my bones. I want to say yes so desperately. I want to live my fantasy of being this dragon's wife and living in his castle with him, but my mind won't let me.

"I can't. You're too good for me. I mean look at all this. A princess should be living in this castle, not a maid."

"I'll make you a princess, Esmeralda."

"I can't do that to you. I told you I am here to make money to pay my family's debts. Can't you see, I can never be your equal?"

"You're wrong," he says. "I paid your family's debts. Your brother is free now."

"What?"

"I couldn't let the mother of my child worry about trivial things like that." He brushes a lock of hair away from my face. My entire body tingles with the need to be his. I want to belong to this big, beautiful dragon. "You're too precious, baby. I can't let anyone else have you. Resist all you want, but you are going to marry me."

"I...I can't thank you enough for what you've done, but

I'm in your debt." I want to stop denying him too, but I know taking advantage of his generosity isn't right.

"Esmeralda." He places his paw over mine, covering my entire hand. "You don't have to thank me or be grateful. Whatever belongs to me, belongs to you." He pauses, his eyes turning away. "There's something I haven't told you yet."

I raise my eyebrows. Blaze gazes deep into my eyes, leaning forward until his snout is almost touching my lips. His warm breaths make my skin prickle with arousal. "You're my mate."

"What?" I gasp, reeling back with shock. It's like he's splashed cold water on me. I know what mates mean to dragons. Dragons can only breed with their mates and they're most compatible with them. Blaze has waited his entire life to find his mate. "It...can't be...how can I be your mate?"

"When I was young, an astrologer prophesied that my mate would knock over the love potion. That is how I would know that we were meant to be. He gave me that blue liquid which has been lying around in my room for a century. Many maids have come and gone, but nobody has ever broken it. I waited for years for someone to break the curse. When you finally knocked over the glass, I knew that you were the one I was meant to find."

My heart hammers in my chest, disbelief coloring my brain. "Oh my god..." If what he's saying is right then...I'm a dragon's mate! "But that was just an accident."

"A fated accident. We were always meant to meet." His finger caresses my hand, making goosebumps rise over the surface of my skin. Only he can reduce me to a fevered mess of emotions with just one touch. "You feel it too, don't you?

That's why you stared at me while I was bathing. You felt a connection."

"Yes." I don't deny it. My system is still struggling to process that I'm this majestic dragon's mate. It's like a dream come true. Now that I think about it, everything that happened—my attraction to him, breaking the glass, the ease with which he bred me, our perfect chemistry—makes sense.

"That is why I must marry you," he says, taking my hand in his. "You're my mate, little one. Nobody else is right for me. Only you can bear my children and be my partner. Our bodies are perfect together. Our minds are in harmony. We were fated to find each other."

I see it now. I see it clearly. Truth be told, I can never imagine spending my life with anyone but Blaze.

Tears spill from my eyes. "Oh my god, I cannot believe this is true. This is...beyond what I hoped for."

"Say yes, love," he says in his deep voice. "Tell me you'll marry me and be mine."

"Yes," I affirm in a low voice. "I will marry you, Blaze. I will spend the rest of my life serving you and making you happy."

Blaze crushes his lips to mine before I can begin crying in earnest. My heart is so full of joy that I fear it might not lost. I've never had anything or anyone in life who made me feel so precious, but Blaze is like a gift from the heavens. I cling to him, my fingers digging into his scaly back. I open my mouth for him and let him nibble on my human lips with his big teeth. When he's ready for more, I take his tongue into my mouth and taste his raw, masculinity. I wish I could preserve this moment forever.

When our lips part, Blaze says, "Thank you, my mate. I will always treasure you. We'll have a big wedding so that everyone knows you're mine." His fingers touch my stomach, kissing down my throat. His warm breath on my skin makes me feel safe and needed. "Though everyone will know soon because you'll start showing."

"I love you." I cry, my tears becoming sobs. Blaze puts his hands around me and lifts me up from the chair, cradling me in his lap.

"Shhh...don't cry." His snout kisses my cheek, rubbing some wetness over it. "I'm here now. We're going to be together, darling."

"I still can't believe it. I love you so much it hurts. I've been driving myself crazy for the last three days, trying to deny what I feel. I want you so bad, but I don't want you to feel cheated."

"Esmeralda, I don't feel cheated at all. On the other hand, I'm the one enjoying all the pleasures in this relationship."

"But...there's nothing I can give you except my love," I say. "My body, my soul, my heart are all yours. But I don't have anything of value."

"You are the most valuable thing to me, little girl. No amount of wealth or status can ever make me feel the way you do." His voice is soft and gentle. "Your love is all I need."

I'm so lucky that Blaze has such a generous heart. The waterworks begin, but Blaze meticulously wipes my tears until I calm down. His fingers slip under my skirt, caressing my thigh, and my pussy reacts. I hold him and finish crying until all the sorrow in my heart is gone and the realization that I'm his mate has sunk in.

"I still can't believe we're mates. I always felt you were special, but I didn't dare hope for more."

"I knew it too. It was torture just watching you and not

getting to touch you. Every time I watched your hips move, I wanted to throw you down on the floor and breed you."

"You watched me?" I ask, surprised. "I thought I was the only one holding a torch for you."

"I watched you all the time. Part of me already knew that you were the one, but I had to wait to make sure." He picks me off and stands up. "Let's go back to our bedroom. I can't wait to take that red gown off you and make love to you."

I smile, needing his touch on my skin more than anything. "I'm all yours."

CHAPTER 4
BLAZE

I'm standing next to my wife, who looks radiant in a silvery white gown on our wedding day. The full sleeves slide over her arms, the A-line design hugging her ample bosom and fanning around her wide hips. My wings unfurled, and I stand by my mate's side during the wedding ceremony. Her warm eyes are gazing at me with love. Every time I see her, I am even more sure of my decision. I am so glad I finally met my fated partner.

Before us are a mix of humans and dragons who have come to attend our wedding at the castle. My staff is busy, supplying food, guiding guests, and maintaining an overall atmosphere of cheer. Esmeralda's family is sitting in the front row, her brother, mother, and father dressed in grand clothes that I made sure they had. I want Esmeralda to have the most grand wedding, even though she said she'd be happy marrying me anywhere. Meeting my mate is an assertion of my status as a dragon elite. The most powerful dragons have come to witness our union, knowing I am ready to do my duty of expanding our population. I have found my mate, and it's a moment of celebration.

"Do you take Esmeralda to be your lawfully wedded wife?" The priest asks me. I gaze down at my human wife who barely reaches my hip. She's beautiful with her brown hair pinned back in an intricate bun. We decided to get married within a month of my proposal before she started showing. I'm excited to start this new phase of my life with Esmeralda by my side. She loves me for who I am, and that's all I've ever wanted.

"Yes." My deep voice rumbles in the castle, eliciting a round of applause from the pews. Despite our huge size difference, we are perfect together.

"Do you take Blaze to be your lawfully wedded husband?" The priest turns to my glowing mate. She takes my breath away whenever I look at her. A cool gold and diamond necklace rests on her bosom—my wedding gift to her. I'm going to spoil my mate for the rest of my life, and it's time she got used to it.

Her deep brown eyes meet mine. Her soft pink lips part and say the words I want to hear. "Yes."

Thunderous applause follows, and we are joined in matrimony before an audience. I feel joyful as flowers rain down on us.

We've become one. The whole world knows Esmeralda is mine now. There's no better feeling.

EVENING LIGHTS FILTER through the huge windows of the castle. My hands are tucked around Esmeralda's hips, watching over the row of my staff gathered in front of me. I've ordered all of them to gather at the main entrance to get to know their mistress. I can feel my wife trembling against me, chewing her bottom lip nervously. She used to be one of my servants before I made her my wife, and it makes her apprehensive.

"Do you think they'll accept me as their mistress?" she asked me earlier while I undid her wedding gown after the ceremony. "What if they hate me for seducing the master?"

"You didn't seduce me, my wife." I kissed her lips. "I was meant to find you."

I am determined to show her that we can have a happy life here in my castle. My fifty human servants turn their heads up, waiting for my next words.

"I thank you all for your hard work in preparing for our wedding," I open. "As a bonus, you will all receive a month's salary. My wife has also prepared a feast for you in the gardens as a reward."

Cheers echo in the castle as my staff beam at my generosity. "Thank you, ma'am."

Esmeralda smiles at my staff, her body pressed to mine. "I thought you all deserved it."

I turn to my wife. I hold her hand, feeling her slip her fingers around my thick thumbs. "This will be a welcome dinner for my wife. Esmeralda is your new mistress. I hope you will treat me here with the same reverence and respect that you accord to me. Anyone who doesn't will have to face my wrath."

My final words are laced with a warning.

Esmeralda turns to the staff and smiles. "Thank you for accepting me as your mistress. I will endeavor to be kind and fair to everyone here. In exchange, I ask for your loyalty and respect."

She sounds more confident now. I've broken down her resistance and she has begun to acknowledge that she's finally a dragon's bride.

"Welcome to the castle, mistress." The staff echo

together, a few of them congratulating Esmeralda on our marriage. It's a warmer welcome than both of us expected. They're all excited to have a new mistress, even if it is one of them. Once my heir is born, Esmeralda's position will further be cemented in my household.

My human wife and I guide our staff to the feast outside. After making sure they're enjoying it, we retire to our bedroom for our first night together as husband and wife.

I push Esmeralda onto the bed before she can speak, throwing her skirts up.

"Blaze!" She opens her legs willingly for me, enjoying my attention.

"Now that my staff are busy eating, it's time I feasted on my new wife." I part her legs to gaze at that perfect pink pussy, all wet and ready for me. "You're wet, my love."

"Mmmm...I've been around my hot dragon husband all day. My poor pussy is weeping for attention." The glow in her eyes makes my heart swell. She wants me. Esmeralda begins undoing the buttons on her wedding gown, popping them one by one to reveal her undergarments. I wait patiently while she takes them off, not wanting to ruin her wedding dress. It's a special memento, a symbol of our love.

Placing it aside, she presents me with her naked body. The sight of my fertile human wife takes my breath away. She extends her arms and I come to her, holding her close. "I'm yours," she whispers. "I can't believe we're married."

"You're all I've wanted," I say, my hands sliding over her stomach and cupping her mound that's covered with dark hair. I slip under it, finding her fleshy folds and rubbing them with my fingers. "I'm going to keep you in bed all night."

She smiles. "I can't wait."

I press on her tiny clit and she cries out, pressing her breasts against my scaly torso. The friction makes her hotter, her pussy gushing liquid in response. I want to taste her honey. I kiss a trail down her body, burying my snout in her breasts and her stomach. Pressing a hot kiss on her soft belly, I whisper, "Soon, this stomach will be swollen with your baby. I can't wait until you're pregnant, Esmeralda. I'm going to enjoy breeding you with a baby baking in your stomach. You'll look so hot and fertile with your big belly bouncing while your dragon mate breeds you."

"Mmmmm..." She moans, caressing my head. "You always make me feel so good."

I slip my huge snout between her legs, the scent of her pussy drugging me. "Damn, your pussy smells so sweet." My thick, forked tongue emerges, licking my wife's folds. She arches her back, her fleshy thighs closing around my head.

"Oh my god, Blaze..."

"I'm just getting started, baby." I leisurely lick her folds from clit to asshole, devouring her flavor. She tastes so sweet like she's mine. When my tongue flicks on her aching bud, she begins to shake. I circle her dripping cunt, circling her quivering hole. "I'm going to eat your pussy, princess, and then, I'm going to breed you all night."

My long tongue thrusts into her hole. My wife's cries fill my chamber. "Blaze...oh my god...your tongue is so thick." My forked tongue plugs up her pussy, slithering inside her wet, fleshy channel. I scissor her stuffed cunt, teasing her sweet spot. Honey drips on my tongue as her arousal peaks.

"Your pussy tastes so sweet, wife. I want to lap up every last drop of moisture." I thrust my tongue in and out of her channel, filling it and stretching it again and again. The taste of her pleasure bleeding onto my tongue is the best thing ever.

"Don't stop..." she cries, shaking under me as I thrust my tongue in and out of her delicious pussy, licking her insides. The tension builds in her core until she can't take it anymore. "I'm going to come."

My wife breaks apart with a loud cry while I continue thrusting my tongue inside her needy hole. An orgasm sweeps her up, making her surrender to her monster husband. Esmeralda's silky walls massage my tongue. Her entire body spasms, the contractions inside her pussy driving me wild with desire. My cock is hard and needy, aching to penetrate my wife's tight channel. I pull my tongue out of her and replace it with my cock. My huge organ slides into her pussy, stretching her walls to the max and heightening her orgasm.

"Blaze!" My wife's cries grow louder as my little human lets me use her body to bring myself pleasure. The feeling of that tight pussy gripping my purple monster cock makes my body burn.

"My sweet, little wife. I love how you milk my dick with your fertile pussy." The rippling of her walls all around my shaft is pure torture. I begin thrusting into her, slamming deep into her orgasming womb and hitting her cervix. Our bodies are made for each other, her vice-like grip bringing me immense pleasure. Wet sounds of fucking fill the air. The need in my belly pulses out of control just before it explodes into a climax. My growl emanates in the room when we come together as a dragon and wife for the first time. I push my knot into her, locking into her pussy and spewing my cum all over her unprotected walls. My mate's pussy milks me, nurturing my cum inside.

It is the most perfect feeling in the world.

When the orgasm slows down, I gaze at my naked wife panting under me.

"Blaze...oh..." I'm still knotted inside her pussy, filling her with my baby-making batter. Esmeralda reaches up and kisses me, dropping kisses all over my mouth and jaw, and even my eyelids. "I love you so much, my husband."

"Me too," I say, holding her close. Our sweaty bodies slide over each other, revering and worshipping in nakedness. "You're mine now."

As I hold her close, my fingers playing with her soft tits, I observe her gaze wander to the closed room attached to my chamber.

"What is that?" she asks. "I know the maids weren't allowed to go in there."

"My hoard," I tell her. "That's where I collect all my precious baubles. Do you want to have a look?"

"I...I couldn't. I know dragon hoards are precious."

"You're my wife now," I say, putting my hands under her ass and squeezing those round globes of flesh. Her muscles squeeze my cock that's still inside her. My mate wraps her legs around me as I pull both of us off the bed and carry her to my treasure trove. I unlock the door with my nail. Only dragon nails work on that lock.

My wife is snug on my cock, her arms around me, her hair around her naked body when we enter my hoard. The moment the gold and glitter hits her eyes, her jaw drops.

"Oh my god...this is...like a city of gold."

All around us are mountains of gold coins, gold bars, silver crockery, and thousands of gems—emeralds, rubies, sapphires, and diamonds. It's my treasure trove, filled with all the precious objects that I've accumulated over my lifetime. There are crystal glasses, an odd crystal ball or two, and even some things of emotional significance those who are indebted to me gave me.

"This is magnificent..." Esmeralda turns to me. "I knew you were rich, but this is beyond anything I imagined. How am I ever supposed to compare to all this beauty and wealth?"

"Look at me." I bring her face to mine, breathing over her hard nipples. "You're the most precious gem in my collection, Esmeralda. These things are mere objects, but your love is invaluable."

She inhales, her eyes softening. "Blaze..."

"Starting today, you're the mistress of this chamber too. You can wear these jewels whenever you want. Only my wife is allowed access to my hoard."

"What..."

"You deserve to be showered with the best, my love." I kiss my naked human bride, loving the way she feels in my arms. Her softness is a contrast to my roughness. "Now that you're my wife, I'm going to spoil you."

"You already spoil me," she says. "You even gave me a diamond necklace at our wedding."

"That's just the beginning," I tell her with a smirk.

CHAPTER 5
ESMERALDA
FIVE MONTHS LATER—

Blaze wasn't lying when he said he was just getting started on spoiling me. The cool air hits my face as I fly through the clear afternoon sky, the sun warming my skin. I'm sitting on my dragon husband's back, hanging onto him as he gives me an aerial tour of the castle. My huge, pregnant stomach bulges in front of me, reminding me that I'm carrying our precious son. We know it's a son because dragons have a way of knowing. Blaze told me early into our pregnancy that we were having a dragon son, and I couldn't be happier. I hope my son is kind and strong like his father. Decked in an emerald necklace and matching earrings, I'm being serenaded early in the morning.

"This is beautiful. I've never seen the castle from up here."Acres of lush green trees soothe my eyes. There's a stream at the edge of Blaze's estate, complete with a waterfall. Blaze has been taking care of me ever since we got married. I wake up in bed with my favorite dragon every day, submitting to pleasure. Over our time together, my love for my dragon master has only grown. With our child coming soon, he wants us to strengthen that bond. That's why he's taking me out. "That waterfall looks so cool."

"That's where I bathe," Blaze says, flapping his large wings. His wingspan is impressive. I touch his wings, making him shudder. I know how sensitive he is there, and I love making him all hot and hungry for my body. Blaze has been really into fucking me ever since I started to show. He loves my pregnant body so much that we end up spending most of our time indoors, making love.

He begins to descend, moving closer to the waterfall and stream. I touch his scaly skin, loving the way his muscles ripple under my hand. My pussy clenches when his tail slips up behind me, stroking the patch of skin on my back. I'm wearing a loose gown with a deep-cut neck and back. Most of my usual clothes stopped fitting me when I started to show, so Blaze ordered new ones. However, the garments can't contain my growing tits and bulge. My breasts spill out from the top, my nipples straining under the hem.

Blaze's feet hit the ground as he lands near the stream. My eyes take in the lush green grass, the trees, and the flowing clear water around us. I climb off my mate's back, my bare feet touching the cool grass. My body instantly feels calm and tingly. Blaze's wings collapse. He comes to stand before me, gazing down at my pregnant body.

"You're so beautiful, my fertile wife." His thick fingers stroke my cheek. "Pregnancy makes your body look even more stunning. All these lush curves, this beautiful soft, fat..." His digits trail down my body, caressing my overflowing tits before curving around my round stomach. His big fingers encompass by baby bump, stroking it gently. His touch makes my pussy contract, aching for nearness. "I want to keep you pregnant forever."

My fingers join his on my stomach. I'm so happy to be nourishing my dragon master's seed inside my womb. I can't wait to meet our son. When Blaze's fingers brush the curve of my massive tits, I feel a sudden ache in my boobs. They have been feeling tender since morning, though I assumed that was just the pregnancy hormones. But as Blaze continues stroking my belly and tits, I feel a pressure building behind my nipples. When I wince, Blaze asks, "What's wrong, my love?"

"Nothing." I automatically reply, not wanting to worry him. My palms touch his hand soothingly. "I'm just sensitive because of my pregnancy."

"Carrying a dragon baby is a lot of work," Blaze says. "I hope you're eating well."

"You feed me all the time," I say. "I weigh as much as a house thanks to all the luxurious food I've been consuming."

"You need it, baby." He leans lower, his snout brushing on my temple. "It's my job to keep you well-fed and well-pleasured. After all, you're carrying our baby, and that isn't an easy task. You deserve to be pampered for being such a good, pregnant wife." I can feel his rough fingers skimming my almost naked breasts, brushing the tops of my swollen orbs. His touch worsens the ache in my chest, and I feel something wet under my dress. Blaze's eyes widen as two wet spots form on my gown, right where my nipples are supposed to be.

Horrified, I jump back. "What's that?"

"It must be the milk coming in early." My dragon husband steps closer. "Your body is getting ready to nourish our baby. God, you're such a sexy mother."

I'm lactating. I can't believe it. I never thought I'd be producing milk so early, but my body already knows my baby is going to come. Blaze's yellow eyes are filled with hunger when he looks at me. "Come here, little human. Let me see your motherly body."

"Here?" I ask, shocked. "We're outside."

"Your body belongs to me, little wife, no matter where we are. And I want to see my mate's pregnant form. Naked"

Shivers run up my spine at the naughty request. I've never been naked under the sky, in a place where anyone could stumble on us. Part me of wants to strip naked for him and see his eyes light up with lust. I want to let him breed me right here on the grass next to the stream. But another naughty part of me wants to play with my baby daddy. I know how much my dragon husband loves chasing. It's in his primal nature to chase and conquer, and today, I'm going to let him conquer me.

I take a step back, picking up my skirt. "You want to look at me naked?" My legs buzz with energy, ready to run. "You'll have to catch me first."

With that, I take off running. My tits hurt as they bounce with every step, my huge pregnant belly wobbling. I hear Blaze's growl piece the air and then, he's after me, chasing me down like the predator he is. I run through the lush grass, struggling to keep pace due to my swollen belly and aching tits. My udders leak milk, wetting my gown even more. I hold my pregnant belly in my hand, steadying it as I run further into the woods.

"Come here, wife. You know I'm going to catch you." My precious dragon mate flies through the thicket of trees, his breath echoing in the air. I'm struggling to run, to keep pace with the much larger creature following me, but I don't want to give in yet. Branches break under my bare feet as I venture deeper, running close to the stream. I can feel how close he is to me, feel his sharp nails cutting the air.

THE DRAGON'S MAID

"Esmeralda." His growl is the last thing I hear before he catches me.

My legs stop moving, being pulled off the ground by a huge, lying dragon. Blaze's scales gleam as he carries me over the trees to the stream where we got off. I cry out loud, pushing and kicking in his firm arms, but it's no use. My dragon's tail curves under my skirt, creeping up between my legs to find my pussy that's always horny for my husband.

"Stop resisting, little one. Your pussy is so wet for me." The tip of his tail runs over my wet seam. The ache in the breasts worsens. My tits spew milk in arousal, drenching the front of my dress. Beads of dew coat my slit. Blaze places me on the ground, his tail still playing with my pussy. His fingers rip my new gown into shreds, claiming his prize.

The restrictive bodice disappears, releasing my engorged, bare tits. They spill over like two firm melons. My pink tips are elongated and sensitive, coated with beads of white milk. My pregnant body is naked, yards of creamy skin presented for my husband's eyes only. The cool wind and spray of water hit my baby bump from the side.

"So beautiful..." Blaze places his hands over my swollen stomach. He bends down and kisses my swollen womb, licking my skin. My tits fountain milk in response to his touch which makes my body go hot and needy. "You're so horny, my milky wife." He sticks out his long tongue and laps up a bead of milk from my aching teat. The feeling of his hot, wet tongue on my nipples makes me cry out in shock.

"Mmmm...so sweet...." His tail circles my quivering cunt, slipping into my wet hole. I cry out louder when he stretches me. "Look how gorgeous you are, your stomach all swollen with my baby, those hips thick and fleshy, and those teats leaking milk. Your fertile mama body is a sight to behold. All these supple curves and those massive, milky tits...so perfectly round with the most lickable nipples." His tongue leisurely rolls over my other nipple, steadily leaking cream for him, lapping up the sweetness. Every time his tongue flicks my bead, it feels so good. My full udders are crying out for release. "I'm obsessed with your knocked-up body, my human wife."

"Yes...please, drink from my tits. They ache so bad for your mouth."

Blaze leans forward, his thick cock swelling and hardening at the sight of my naked body. I can feel his meat next to my pregnant stomach, proof of his virility. My body shudders, heat pooling between my legs and taking my dragon master's tail even deeper. He curves his large palm around my tits, and gently squeezes them, slowly massaging milk from my aching tips.

"Oh my god...that feels so good." I place my hand over him, loving him touching my udders. When he leans down and puts his large snout to my tips, my pussy clenches around his tail. His hot mouth latches onto my tip and sucks hard.

"Aaahhh..."

Milk streams out of my tits, hitting the back of Blaze's mouth. The letdown sends a spiral of relief through my body. Blaze's tail moves inside my pussy, thrusting in and out and teasing my clenching walls.

He sucks another mouthful of cream, draining my tit steadily. His hands are on my tit, squeezing them, milking them, rolling my lonely nipple around, and making shocks of pleasure rocket through my system.

I love being milked by my dragon husband. I never

thought it'd feel so good, but a huge dragon milking my tits, deriving nourishment from my tiny human body fills me with so much joy. I want to take care of Blaze like he takes care of me, and right now, the only way I can do that is by offering him my sweet titty milk. Putting my hand over his scaly purple head, I touch his little ears and caress his rough skin.

"Drink as much as you want," I coo. "I love feeding you."

His mouth tightens around my peak, sucking harder while his tail winds out of my pussy. He removes his hand from my full tit and tears his mouth away. Blaze's long tongue licks his lips as his cock grinds into my dripping folds.

Blaze teases my pussy with the dripping tip of his erect cock, depositing lavender pre-cum all over my folds and rubbing it in. "Ummm..." A fire burns in my belly. "I need your cock," I beg. "Please, fill me up while your baby is inside me and remind me who bred me so well and made my stomach swell."

Blaze's hungry growl echoes in the air. I can hear the water from the stream, and feel the soft grass under my back, but all I need right now is my husband's monster cock, knotting me and plugging me up while he sucks my massive milkers like a baby.

"Damn, you're a fertile goddess, Esmeralda." Blaze plants milky kisses all over my full breasts and swollen stomach. "I want to knock you up again, baby, you look so perfect with my seed growing inside you." My body lights up at his compliment, my pussy feeling every slide of his cock on my folds. Blaze pushes my legs apart and stares at my wet hole, hissing with need. His cock is thick and fat, big and ready to penetrate me. He pushes the tip of his penis inside my cunt, diving in deeper and deeper. "Damn it, you're so tight. I love this pussy so much." He leans over, massaging milk over my pregnant stomach as his mouth finds my full teat. He latches onto it and sucks hard, making my pussy squeeze his erection. With a wild cry, I take him in deeper, loving the delicious stretch as my pussy swallows his dick. When he's fully inside me, I squeeze my legs together, making his cock twitch inside me. He bites my nipple, making the pressure inside my core skyrocket. Milk splashes his big mouth and he drinks it down hungrily. "Damn, you're choking me already, little wife. I need that slutty pussy grasping me while I suckle your cream."

His teeth graze my tender nipple, making me wild with desire. His tail pushes up, playing with my clit, flicking it and rolling it like a marble. Blaze begins thrusting into my hole, his big balls slapping my ass as he squelches in and out of my intimate passage. He pounds my tender flesh like a drum, making sparks burst everywhere in my body. At the same time, his mouth covers my teat and sucks hard. He steadily suctions my breast with wet sounds, his hands loving my pregnant stomach while his cock drills me ruthlessly. I can't resist the pressure that's begging to explode. My fleshy cavern ripples over his cock, loving the way his cock scrapes against my bare walls. He owns my pussy, owns me, and the proof is in my stomach right now.

"I'm going to come!" I can barely hear my voice, the pleasure, Blaze's growls, and the cool air weaving a spell on me. His cock hits the entrance of my womb, claiming the vessel he planted his seed in, and I unravel.

"Come for me, mate." He says, pushing his knot into my hole. I can't take it anymore. I short-circuit with a loud cry. My entire body is gripped by shockwaves of bliss as my climax explodes. My pussy spasms around my dragon husband's purple dick, milking that monster for all it's worth.

"Damn, baby, I'm coming." Blaze's cock locks into place, drenching my well-bred walls with cum. His mouth steadily suctions from my tits, alternating between my sore teats, licking and teasing them until they're empty. When he sucks my nipple and nothing comes out, he tears his mouth away with a wild cry, pumping me full of cum. He keeps rutting into me, emptying his balls with wild thrusts. "You're so sexy when you come, Esmeralda. I love how your tits and that big stomach jiggle. If your belly wasn't full with a baby already, I'd fuck one right into you."

We rock into each other, riding out our orgasms joined as one. I'm all bred and drained, my pregnant belly possessively clutched by my dragon husband, and my naked body knotted on the grass. He's conquered me thoroughly.

When my eyes open, all I see is his beautiful, purple countenance, and those golden eyes that make my heart melt. His cock pulses inside my channel, my swollen stomach resting against his golden mid-section. Blaze holds me close, kissing my sore breasts and licking each tip soothingly.

"That was incredible," I say. "I've never been made love to outside. You really spoil me."

"That's what I'm here for," he says, licking the last of my milk. "And you're spoiling me with your milk too. I love the sweet cream your body makes, Esmeralda."

"It's yours," I say. "You can have it until the baby is here."

"Dragon babies don't drink milk, Esmeralda." Blaze licks my tit. "But their daddies do." My body is heating up. I am looking forward to more milking sessions with my husband. "You know I'm going to take you non-stop now, don't you? How will I ever be able to resist those milky mounds? God, they're so beautiful. Everything about you is beautiful, my mate. I'm so lucky I found you."

"As am I," I tell him. "I couldn't ask for a better companion. You're always there for me. I've never once felt neglected during my pregnancy."

"You're the center of my world, Esmeralda. I'm going to give you lots of babies, and every time your body is swollen with my seed, we're going to come here and I'm going to make love to you by the stream."

"Deal." I smile, looking forward to more pregnancies. This one has been surprisingly easy thanks to my dragon husband.

"Why don't we take a bath together?" He asks. I nod and seconds later, I'm being carried to the stream on my husband's cock, feeling him securely inside me. The cool water hits both of us, submerging me up to my neck. Blaze kisses me as he tenderly bathes my pregnant body, taking care of the bump. He kisses me, that hot gaze melting my heart. "I love you, baby. I'm so glad you're mine."

I kiss him back, bracketing his protruding mouth with my hands. "I love you too, husband. I'm so proud to call you my mate. You're all I ever wanted, and this baby growing inside my stomach is a testament to our love."

We kiss each other, this time, deeply.

I close my eyes and let myself be cared for, my husband's cock inside me and his arms around me.

It feels like home.

CHAPTER 6
ESMERALDA
ONE YEAR LATER—

"Come to Mama, Elro." I run after my baby dragon son in the garden, the servants watching on. My baby boy is a little purple dragon just like his Daddy. He's only eight months old, yet, he can already walk. Blaze has been teaching him to fly and he loves practicing.

"Mama...mama..." he says, as I catch him mid-air. I'm glad he can't fly high yet. I won't be able to catch him so easily once he starts doing that.

My son's little arms go around me as I hold him close to my bosom. It's filled with milk, but Elro can't drink it. I kiss his little ears, his bald head that's just beginning to develop scales, and caress his wings, my heart bursting with love for my baby dragon.

"You did so well, baby. You flew really high today. I'm sure Daddy is going to be proud."

"Yes...yes..." He can't say a lot of words, but I hope he understands what I say. He keeps the staff busy with his high energy. I squeeze my little bundle of joy, watching him raise his head from my chest and gaze into my eyes. He's the most perfect baby in the world. I delivered him after ten hours of labor. Though my pregnancy was easy, the labor was hard because he'd grown too big inside my human womb. However, thanks to dragon healers, magical potions, and a lot of encouragement and kisses from Blaze, I managed to give birth to our son. He's the most precious thing in our lives.

"I love you, baby. You're always going to be my number one." I press a kiss to his little nose at the end of his snout. "But you've got to stop flying out of our nursery while I'm sleeping."

He laughs, and my heart melts, forgiving him already.

"I'm sorry, ma'am." A human maid emerges from behind me. She's Elro's nurse. "I shouldn't kept a better eye on the young master."

"He's a dragon," I say. "He loves the outdoors and the blue skies. Just like his Daddy."

Elro, Blaze, and I are a happy little family, and it seems that we're going to be growing soon. After I gave birth, Blaze gave me some time to recover. He's been drinking my milk, but humans need at least eight months to recover from a dragon's baby's birth. It's been torture for him to not breed me, and I've missed having my dragon Daddy's cock inside my pussy. However, we've had to get creative and I've learned to suck dragon dick in the meanwhile.

"Did someone say, Daddy?" Blaze descends from the sky, and instantly my nipples tighten. They're all full and tender, bubbling with milk at the sight of the sexiest dragon alive. My majestic monster materializes, his purple scales shining. His eyes are all for me, making my pussy clench with need. Our dry period is over. Starting today, the dragon healer cleared me for sex. I can't wait to deliver the news to him.

"Elro." Blaze reaches forward and picks up our son, cradling him. He rocks him in his arms, making gurgling noises that Elro enjoys. My mate bounces him around, throwing him up in the air and catching him. Elro's laughter grows wild. He enjoys playing with his Daddy, and I love that Blaze always makes time for us. He's the best father in the world, providing for our son and caring for him.

When Elro begins to get drowsy, and his energy is depleted, he yawns.

"He's sleepy." I place a hand on my dragon's back, the touch sending heat spiraling through both our bodies. Thanks to the months of denial, we're both horny all the time. Tonight, I'm going to put him out of his misery.

Blaze holds a yawning Elro in his arms, rocking him to sleep. When his eyes close, his breath steady, he hands him to the nurse, who carries him to his bedroom. When she leaves, Blaze places his arm around my waist, which is much wider than it used to be, but my husband loves me like this. "How is my wife today?" His eyes skim lower to my inflated bosom, scenting the nutty milk in the air. "Do you need to be milked, Esmeralda?"

"Yes. I've been waiting for you to get home. Take me to our bed, Blaze."

My mate grabs me and in seconds, we're flying in through our bedroom window. I've gotten used to him coming and going through the wide, arched space. He places me on the bed and shuts the window, his hulking form climbing over me. When his snout brushes my full tits, I caress his head, and say, "The dragon healer was here today. I have some news for you."

He pulls the neck of my gown down, making my engorged tits bounce free. My round, milky globes hang heavy, my rosy tips leaking white fluid. He licks the milk off my nipple, making my pussy drip honey. "What did she say?"

"I'm ready to be bred again," I hold his head close as he laps up my cream like a cat, playing with my nipple with that forked tongue. The edges of his tongue wrap around my bud and roll it, making me arch my back with a whimper.

"What?" His eyes meet mine, the realization sinking in. Blaze retracts his tongue. "Do you mean...?"

"Yes." My face is filled with joy. "You can come inside me tonight. Breed me like I know you love to. My pussy is all yours."

"Fuck." I feel his meaty shaft rest against my thigh, ready to drive home. "You're serious, aren't you?"

"I am. I need you, husband. I need that monster cock inside me, filling my pussy with hot cum."

"Oh my god, Esmeralda." His fingers undo my fussy strings and buttons, dying to get me naked. "I love you so much, baby, but not touching your pussy for months was sheer torture."

"I know," I say, kissing his mouth. "I'm so glad we can be together again."

In seconds, Blaze has my clothes off. His fingers play with my full tits, suckling cream and soothing my achy nipples with his tongue while his cock finds my pussy.

"You're so wet, Esmeralda."

"I need you," I cry out. "I need you cock owning my pussy."

"Darling, that's what I've been waiting for."

In one stroke, he impales my pussy, driving home.

"Oh my god..." Pleasure skewers my body as Blaze's

cock re-familiarizes itself with my pussy. I'm not as tight as I used to be, but he's so huge that it's still a stretch.

"God, you're so hot and perfect, wife. I missed being in your pussy so much."

He rocks his hips into my cavern, tugging and pulling on my nipples while he pounds my pussy raw. His thrusts are strong and forceful, aching with the need to take. I know he's missed me, and I love it when he grinds into my fleshy walls with that hard dick, scraping against my womb. "I want to put a baby inside your belly so bad. This perfect pussy was created to be bred by your dragon mate."

"Yes..." I cry out, seeing stars behind my eyes when his dick touches my sweet spot. "Give me your seed, Blaze. Make me come."

It barely takes ten seconds of raw fucking before he's knotting me and filling my belly with his hot cum. I orgasm on his cock, drenching him in my juices as he plants his seed inside my womb. I love the feeling of hot cum trickling inside me, my dragon husband bare cock plugging me up. I climax so hard that the walls shake with my cries. My adorable monster comes inside me, filling me again and again until his big balls are empty. I cling to him, enjoying how his mouth tugs on my milky teats and suckles them dry.

We both collapse on the bed, his knot inside me seconds later. He licks the last drops of cream from my huge tits, weighing the heavy globes of flesh in his big palms. His lips kiss a trail up my neck and deposit my forbidden milk right on my mouth. I lick my lips, tasting Blaze and my nourishing cream. Our lips mate together in a hot kiss, our bodies joined. This moment is so perfect. I'm never going to get tired of how it feels to have him buried inside me.

When our lips part, Blaze is cupping my ass possessively. "I love you, Esmeralda. The day you broke that glass, you changed my life. Thanks to you, I now have Elro, and the family and love I only ever dreamed of. You've made me whole, my mate, and I'm going to love you for the rest of my life."

"I love you." My eyes fill with tears. I have a home, a family, and most of all, I have his love. "You've given me everything I hold dear, and I will be your wife, the mother of your children, and your precious gem forever. I'm so glad I decided to be a dragon's maid."

He laughs. "From maid to mate to Elro's mommy. We have had a wild journey together, haven't we, love?"

I smile. "I'm sure more adventures await us."

"Oh, I look forward to them."

Life is never dull with my dragon husband by my side. I lay my head on his chest, falling asleep to the beat of his heart.

ABOUT THE AUTHOR

Jade Swallow is an author of super steamy novels. She loves reading and writing filthy tales featuring all kinds of kinks. Follow her on Instagram @authorjadeswallow for news about upcoming books.

Sign up for my newsletter here to get updates about my upcoming releases: subscribepage.io/eiSMM1

Also by Jade Swallow

Want to read more in this series? Check out these books in the Married and Pregnant Monster Shorts series:

The Sea God's Fertile Bride : An age gap tentacle monster erotica (Married and Pregnant Monster Shorts #1)

Beauty and the Orc: An age gap orc daddy monster romance (Married and Pregnant Monster Shorts #2)

Looking for paranormal and omegaverse erotica? Check out these books by me:

Stranded on the Shifter's Mountain: A Fated Mates Werewolf Shifter Romance with Breeding and Pregnancy

A Hucow Nanny for the Alpha Daddies: An age gap reverse harem fated mates omegaverse novella with pregnancy and milking (Omegaverse Daddies #1)

Alpha Daddy's Omega: An age gap pregnancy knotting and pregnant short story with arranged marriage (Omegaverse Daddies #2)

Love Daddy kink, breeding, and milking? Check out these books:

Breeding the Babysitter: A forbidden age gap billionaire romance with pregnancy (Forbidden Daddies #1)

Mountain Daddy's Curvy Maid : A grumpy-sunshine age gap romance with pregnancy and lactation (Mountain Daddies #1)

Pregnant by the Mafia Boss : A forbidden age gap mafia romance with pregnancy (Mafia Daddies #1)

Claiming my Ex's Dad: A forbidden age gap erotica

Milked by my Best Friend's Mom : An age gap lesbian erotic novella

Short story bundles:

Summer Heat Series Bundle (Summer Heat #1-5)

Feeding Fantasies Box Set (Feeding Fantasies 1-5 + 2 bonus shorts)

A Hucow Maid for the Billionaire (Billionaires & Hucows #1)

Love dark college romances with steam and plot? Check out this one:

Broken (Twisted Souls #1)

She's a serial killer on a mission, and he's her next target. But things get complicated when she begins falling for him...